BEARNARD'S
BOOK

For YOU,
just the way you are —D. U.

For the children at the
Lincoln School Extended Day Program
in Brookline —M. S.

Henry Holt and Company, *Publishers since 1866*
Henry Holt® is a registered trademark of Macmillan Publishing Group, LLC
175 Fifth Avenue, New York, NY 10010 · mackids.com

Text copyright © 2019 by Deborah Underwood
Illustrations copyright © 2019 by Misa Saburi
All rights reserved.

ISBN 978-1-62779-757-3
Library of Congress Control Number 2018945005

Our books may be purchased in bulk for promotional, educational, or business use. Please
contact your local bookseller or the Macmillan Corporate and Premium Sales Department
at (800) 221-7945 ext. 5442 or by e-mail at MacmillanSpecialMarkets@macmillan.com.

First edition, 2019 / Designed by April Ward + Sophie Erb
The illustrations for this book were created with Adobe Photoshop.
Printed in China by Hung Hing Off-set Printing Co. Ltd., Heshan City, Guangdong Province

1 3 5 7 9 10 8 6 4 2

BEARNARD'S BOOK

Deborah Underwood
illustrated by Misa Saburi

GODWINBOOKS

Henry Holt and Company
New York

One day, Bearnard received an important letter:

Dear Bearnard,

YOU have been specially selected to be in a book! Please come to Storybook Gate tomorrow at 10 a.m.

Regally yours,
The Queen of Storybook Land

"**At last!**" Bearnard cried.

"I have always wanted to be in a book!"

He imagined children reading his book at bedtime,

and at school,

and upside down on the playground.

He raced to tell his friend Gertie.

"Gertie! I am going to be in a book!"

"Wonderful!" Gertie said. "What kind of book?"

"I don't know!" Bearnard said. "Maybe I will be a knight."

"Or an astronaut . . . or Super Bear!" Bearnard said.

"Whichever it is, I know you'll do a great job," said Gertie.

Bearnard **wanted** to do a great job.

So he decided to study some other bear books.

He read a book about a bear who floated away in an umbrella.

"Oh dear. What if I need to float in my book?" said Bearnard.

"I'm afraid of floating."

He filled up his bathtub to practice.

"What are you doing?" Gertie called.

"Not floating," said Bearnard.

"Maybe you won't need to float in your book," said Gertie.

Bearnard read a book about
a bear who ate marmalade
and made messes.

"I *do* like marmalade," Bearnard said.

"But I'm a tidy bear. Messes make me nervous."

"Just give it a try," said Gertie.

Bearnard threw a tiny scrap of paper on the ground.

He quickly picked it up.

"I'll help," Gertie said. She tossed some peanut shells on the floor.

Bearnard ran for the vacuum cleaner.

"Maybe you won't need to make messes in your book," said Gertie.

Bearnard read a book about a bear whose porridge was stolen.

"How dreadful!" Bearnard cried. "I am *very* afraid of someone eating my porridge!"

He put a bowl of porridge in front of Gertie. "Eat it," he said. "I need to practice."

"Are you sure?" Gertie asked. "You love porridge."

Bearnard nodded.

Gertie took one bite. Then another. She was about to
take a third bite when—
"STOP!" Bearnard said. "I will have just one spoonful."
"Maybe no one will steal porridge in your book," said Gertie.

That night, Bearnard dreamed of a floating,
messy, porridge-stealing monster.

"I have changed my mind," he said the next morning.

"I do NOT want to be in a book."

"Bearnard!" said Gertie.

"You tried to float. You tried to make a mess. You tried to let me eat your porridge.

Do you know what that makes you?"

"What?" asked Bearnard.

"Brave," said Gertie.

"It does?" said Bearnard.

"Yes," said Gertie.

Bearnard took a deep breath.

"Gertie? Can brave bears bring friends along?"

"Absolutely," said Gertie.

Gertie helped Bearnard relax while they walked to Storybook Gate.

At the gate, Bearnard waved goodbye
to Gertie.

"Welcome, Bearnard!" said the queen. "Right this way."

"Thank you," Bearnard said. "Can you please tell me
what my book is about?"

"Why, don't you know?"
asked the queen. "It's about you!"

"It's about ME?"

"Yes," said the queen. "It's about Bearnard the brave bear getting ready to be in his book. All you need to do is be yourself."

"Thank goodness!" said Bearnard. He turned to tell Gertie but remembered she wasn't there.

Then he had an idea. "My friend Gertie helped me get ready. Can she be in my book, too?" he asked.

"Of course," said the queen.

"Hooray!" said Bearnard.

He ran back to get her.

And together Bearnard and Gertie danced into
Brave Bearnard's Book.